Summer Wonders

by Bob Raczka illustrated by Judy Stead

Albert Whitman & Company, Morton Grove, Illinois

Library of Congress Cataloging-in-Publication Data

Raczka, Bob.
Summer wonders / by Bob Raczka ; illustrated by Judy Stead.
p. cm.
Summary: Illustrations and rhyming text celebrate the sights and sounds of summer, from days
of diving and swimming to nights of stargazing and fireflies.
ISBN 978-0-8075-7653-3
[1. Stories in rhyme. 2. Summer—Fiction.] I. Stead, Judy, ill. II. Title.
PZ8.3.R11153Sum 2009 [E]—dc22 2008031037

The design is by Carol Gildar.

For more information about Albert Whitman & Company,
please visit our web site at www.albertwhitman.com.

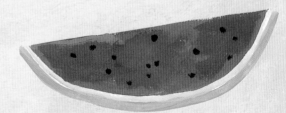

To Carl, my middle guy, who was born in July.—B.R.

To Marguerite Greer, with love and memories of
sunny summer days at Long Beach.—J.S.

Divers,

swimmers,

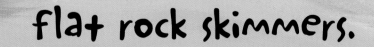

flat rock skimmers.

Joggers,

walkers,

sidewalk chalkers.

Marchers,

pipers,

stars and stripers.

Sliders,

swingers,

picnic bringers.

Readers,

rhymers,

tall-tree climbers.

Growers,   weeders,

melon eaters.

Fanners, sippers,

ice cream drippers.

Combers,

rakers,

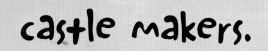
castle makers.

firefliers.

Summer.

# Mini Ice Pops

Did you know the first ice pop was invented almost one hundred years ago by an eleven-year-old boy? It happened by accident. Frank Epperson left his fruit-flavored soda outside with a stirring stick in it, and it froze that way. He called his invention the "Epsicle Ice Pop."

You can make your own Mini Ice Pops. They're easy, they're fun, and you can make any flavor you like.

Here's what you'll need:

- An empty ice-cube tray
- A box of toothpicks (flat ones work best)
- Plastic wrap
- A pitcher of fruit juice or your favorite powdered drink

1. With help from Mom or Dad, carefully fill a clean ice-cube tray with your favorite fruit drink.

2. Cover the ice-cube tray tightly with plastic wrap.

3. Stick a toothpick through the plastic wrap and into the center of each juice-filled "cup."

4. Put the ice-cube tray in the freezer.

5. Wait 2 to 3 hours, or until the juice is frozen.

When the juice is completely frozen, ask Mom or Dad to twist the tray to release the Mini Ice Pops. Then hold them by the toothpicks and slurp away!

The best part is, you'll have plenty to share with your friends!